Halloween Darkness

by
Euryia Larsen

Description

Klaas Zirol

The Sandman, The Lord of Dreams, The Master of Nightmares, King of the Dream Realm... they're all names for who I am and what I am. What they don't say is that I've always been alone. That is until the Fates thought to tease me with what may yet be. My Queen.

Daria Night

I've always been that person in a crowd that was alone. I dreamed of the perfect man but that is all he was, a dream. Then one Halloween he was my dream come true.

Chapter 1

Klaas

Halloween, the one night I can walk around humans in my true form and not worry about who would see me. This is especially true since those silly vampire movies and television shows came out. While I may appear human, the truth was that I was the master of dreams and nightmares and my appearance reflected my realm.

My skin was smooth to the touch but under closer inspection, it was fluid and always in motion from the sands that make dreams possible flowing freely through me. My eyes glowed with my power, appearing in varied reds and oranges. While I appeared as a man, I was not and that much was evident.

Tonight I didn't have to weave my sand around me to mask my power as I enjoyed strolling through neighborhoods watching the children in their glee. Their young dreamscapes flowed freely without the stresses of daily life holding them back. I smiled as I watched them knowing that even their nightmares were filled with youthful energy.

As I enjoyed my stroll, a tinkling laugh could be heard. Entranced by the sound, I looked for its owner. Then I saw her, the one female that played in the dreams of the Sandman. I'd been dreaming about her for more millennia than I could remember. My soul longed for her, my love, my perfect partner.

She was wearing the typical witch costume but her hair was a soft pink color that was an insight into who she was. She wore a smile that captivated me as she passed out candy to all the children at her door.

The more I watched her the easier it was to see the sadness that filled her, despite her smile. I continued to watch her, unable to tear my eyes away, as she looked up and smiled at me. "Is one of these little monsters yours?"

"No, I'm just appreciating the joy in the scene before me as I continue my stroll."

She smiled at me curiously as the last of the children ran off to their next target. "Do you always dress up to stroll around? That can be taken as a little bit creepy." Her teasing laugh made me smile further.

"Halloween has always been a favorite holiday. The joy of children creates a sense of childish freedom. We have so many worries that sometimes I find myself forgetting what that sense of joy feels like. Watching them reminds me. I've been told there are some creatively decorated houses up ahead if you care to join me." My smile was genuine as I found myself hoping she'd say yes.

She looked around tentatively and I could see her nervousness, her unease, in her eyes. I'd finally found her though and I couldn't let her escape me so easily. I held my hands together behind my back as I weaved a bit of dream magic to ease some of her fears. I watched with a hidden smile as she straightened her shoulders before answering, "You know, I think I will. It's a beautiful night for a stroll."

I could still sense her unease despite the magic and truth be told, she had a right to worry. The dreams of men were nightmares waiting to be released on unsuspecting females. Wanting to ease some of her discomfort, I introduced myself while keeping my hands clasped behind my back. "I'm Klaas, thank you for gifting me with your company."

"I'm Daria but everyone calls me Ria," she smiled shyly after locking her front door and joining me.

"Tell me, Daria, why did you choose to be a witch?" I couldn't help but ask.

"Oh, it's just a costume I had that I quickly threw on. I didn't really think about it but wanted to wear something in the holiday spirit while I handed out treats." She turned to look at me, appraising my appearance as she walked backwards. "Your makeup is amazing, are you anyone in particular?"

I smiled at her words, enjoying being with this female. "The Sandman. He's not as television would have you believe. Dreams are powerful whether good or bad. Without dreams there would be chaos without hope, for our dreams go hand in hand with our hopes."

"What about nightmares? Don't they destroy hope by amplifying our fears?"

"Nightmares give us the power to face our fears without true consequence. But, they can become dangerous. The Sandman's job is not only to give us hope through our dreams, but also to control the nightmares before they can consume us."

"You seem to know a lot about this Sandman, but answer me this… does the master of dreams, dream?" As Daria asked

6

this surprising question I could only smile. If she only knew what dreams that I had.

She came to me in the middle of the night as she did whenever I required rest. I wanted her from the first time I saw her. The dreams I had were different from those of humans. The ones I had were a gift from the spinners of fate, for even immortals had a destiny. After many millennia alone, I was dreaming of the one who was destined to be my queen.

In those dreams, I got to know her and I was gifted with her friendship but how could I let myself feel anything more? She was human, mortal. Yet we would flirt and I found myself wishing for more.

Then the dreams simply stopped. There were no more dreams for the Sandman. As time went by I was certain that I would never see her again, much less have her as my Queen.

I found I missed her and often walked among humans with a hope that one day I would see her again and maybe the fates hadn't been cruel to me. Everytime I went to see them, they simply responded with one word, "Patience." What was patience to someone who had lived an eternity? It was a type of cruelty in itself. Each time I went to slumber it became harder and harder to let sleep claim me.

This night was like any other. Peace was elusive. Yet I slowly drifted off to sleep. Finally, I dreamed again, just when all hope was lost to me…

I was walking through a park. There were trees, a pond with a fountain, pasture and walking trails. It was late afternoon in the fall. The air was crisp but not cold. The leaves were turning and there was a nice breeze blowing the already fallen leaves across the path that I was on. As I was looking around and walking I saw someone coming toward me on the path. It was her. She was smiling and walking towards me. We came together in a friendly embrace of old friends and shared a light kiss on the cheek. We walked and talked to catch up with each other. Where we'd been, what we'd been doing, etc.

Our conversation slowly became more intimate as time went by. The setting sun seemed to just hang in the sky not moving. We were talking for hours but the scene had not changed.

It was then that I became aware that this was a dream and that I was asleep in my chambers. I didn't want to wake up but I couldn't help it. I was almost heartbroken from waking and losing the dream. As I laid there I could still feel the path under my feet, feel the breeze and smell the air from the park. I could even hear her voice as she talked to me. I refused to lose her and let sleep claim me again.

I was in the park walking with her again. Our conversation continued to get more intimate. We moved closer as we talked so others would not hear. We both reached out and held hands as we walked. Soon we were arm in arm and we both recognized that we were going to love each other this day. She looked up to me and we stopped on the path and turned toward each other. I reached for her face and took it gently between my hands and held it. She reached up around my neck and pulled me down toward her.

Our lips met in a tentative kiss, almost as if we didn't want to for fear of exploding. We had both wanted this but never dared hope we could have it. Our touch became even more passionate. The kiss was not tentative any longer. She pulled me closer and her mouth opened and invited me in. Our tongues touched and the thrill was electric. It was almost like a static shock on a cold winter day. Our bodies moved together as we kissed. This seemed to go on forever but was only a brief moment.

I looked at the woman I now knew as Daria and smiled. She was so much more beautiful in this reality. "Does the Sandman dream? I think if he didn't that would be a cruel twist of fate, wouldn't you?"

"I do. I wonder what he dreams about. He's this awe-inspiring being with wondrous powers. What hopes would he have?" She asked with a thoughtful look on her face. "I also wonder what he thinks about humans. What I remember of mythology, the gods generally saw humans as disposable creatures."

I couldn't help the smile on my face. Daria was so like the female in my dreams. She was a joy to be around. Her intelligence made conversation stimulating and entertaining. "Well, without humans he wouldn't have a purpose. I imagine he finds humans to be complex and utterly fascinating creatures that one should never underestimate."

"I hope so. That series on television about the Sandman made me sad. The character of Morpheus seemed so alone to me. He was forced to endure the worst of humans. I hope that if the Sandman were real, he thinks better of us and isn't too lonely."

"You have a beautiful heart, Daria," I smiled at her. "I bet he's seen the best and worst in dreams, but I don't think he'd be so easily captured as Morpheus was. His power can't be taken by taking mere objects from him. The human mind struggles with the idea of boundless infinite power. Such a creature wouldn't have been held prisoner in such a way."

"Hmmm," she paused as she was thinking. "I think you're right. The Lord of Dreams and Nightmares is not a simple being bound in the ways men picture. I just hope he knows love and happiness. More than anything I hope he isn't alone. The idea of him being alone for the rest of eternity brings pain to my heart. Everyone, every creature and being, deserves to know love."

I felt myself smile brightly at the incredible female next to me. The fates had blessed me beyond measure. "Thank you for blessing me with your presence, sweet Daria. I wonder what dreams you have. I hope they are filled with such beauty and happiness."

Chapter 2

Daria

I looked at the handsome man that walked next to me. He was gorgeous with his makeup on. I looked at his skin and found myself thinking that the movement I saw almost looked too real to be makeup. Being around him I realized that my fears eased and I was really enjoying our walk.

What I didn't tell him, how could I without sounding crazy, was that I used to dream of him, all the time. That was until I realized being in love with a dream-man wasn't what I wanted. I wanted someone that could hold me and love me back.

That flesh and blood man was hard to find, though. My loneliness was like a black hole that was sucking me into it. I tried to be happy, but I was only wearing a mask. Then he came back to me in my dreams. It was like no time had passed. The kiss we shared was like none I'd ever experienced.

Then it went even further…

No words passed our lips but we knew it was going to happen, finally. Holding hands we turned from the path and walked into the trees. We were looking for a private place. We walked a short distance and pushed through a low hedge. On the other side we came out into a small clearing. It seemed like a room in the woods. As we stood, we saw a hammock strung between two trees near the middle of the space.

We moved to the hammock while we were kissing and embracing. I tried to slow down, to enjoy this time together fully. I didn't know when or if I'd see him again. Our bodies pushed hard against each other. All the passion of flirting was breaking free and over powering us.

The woods and the hammock slowly morphed into my bedroom and I was standing with him in front of me and my bed next to us instead of the hammock. It seemed almost real but I knew this was just a change of location in a dream. I accepted it and sat on the edge of the bed because my knees were too weak to stand. He slowly moved into place in front of me.

As we undressed each other, more skin became available for me to kiss and touch. He pulled me close to him and reached around to unclasp my bra. Pushing me back a little, I shyly watched as he marveled at my body. "Perfection," he whispered.

My nipples were hard and sticking out like pencil erasers. Demanding his attention, begging for it. I gasped as he moved his mouth to my nipple and sucked it in. He licked and sucked on it like it was the best candy in the world while massaging the other one. I had never felt more aroused than I was at that moment. I was in heaven.

He never broke eye contact with me. I straightened up and reached down to my pants and unbuttoned them while pulling the zipper down. This showed him my pretty, lacy pink panties. Before I could push my pants down, he took over and ran his hands down my legs as he removed both my pants and underwear.

I knew he could smell my arousal and see it seeping from my pussy. I watched with hooded eyes as he leaned forward closing the distance so that his mouth was tasting me. The pleasure was overwhelming and better than anything I'd ever dreamed of. I was quivering all over as he used his tongue to taste every bit of arousal my body gave to him.

Just as my orgasm was about to reach its pinnacle, I woke up. I became aware of the bed under me. I remembered my dream and smiled as I laid there not wanting to wake completely as the dream faded with wakefulness. I laid with my eyes closed, ignoring the world, as I soaked in the memory of the dream.

I groaned as I realized I never saw anything more than his powerful chest. I never experienced an orgasm from this man. It still seemed so real but I knew that I'm all alone. Once again loneliness filled my soul and I started to cry softly to myself.

I look at Klaas shyly as I remember the dream from the night before. The coincidence that I dreamed of him, have always dreamed of him, hit me. "Klaas, what would you say if I were to tell you that I've seen you before in my dreams, only you looked human with brown eyes and tanned skin?"

He looked at me wearing a smirk. "I would have to ask what your senses say about that?

I nibbled my lip nervously, as I tried to answer in a way that wouldn't scare him off or make me feel crazier than I did at this moment. "I... um... I honestly don't know."

I watched as he stopped walking and turned to look at me. He took my hand in his before cupping my cheek, "Feel my touch, my warmth. Do I feel like a dream?"

"No, of course not, but I feel like I've known you forever. The memories I have are of dreams, but…"

"My beautiful, Daria," he interrupted as his fingers caressed my skin. "What if I were to tell you that I had those dreams as well? Would you run from me in fear if I were to tell you that who you see right now is who I am?"

My logical common sense was screaming that he was trying to make a fool out of me. My heart and soul were pleading for me to believe him. "You're the Sandman?" I gasped in a whisper. "No, no, no that can't be. This is a cruel joke. It has to be." I pulled my hand away and stepped back as I looked at him, my senses in a panic.

"My name is Klaas Zoril and I'm known to you as the Sandman, but I have been called many different things by many different people." I watched skeptically as he closed the distance between us and took my hands in his. "Let me prove to you that what I tell you is true."

Chapter 3

Daria

I blinked several times as suddenly the world around us dissolved into a large dark room with a dimly lit stage in the back. I rubbed my eyes to make sure I was seeing things clearly. A sound startled me. There on the stage, Klaas stood with a guitar.

No one else entered, it was just the two of us. I watched from across the room. His hands caressed the neck of the guitar sliding from the first fret on down. He tested the sound, striking chords, tilting his head as he did this, making any tuning adjustments necessary. His eyes closed as he listened.

I realized right then, this instrument was more than just something that created music. It was a work of art, something cherished, something treasured, something adored. From the way he treated his guitar, I could tell he would treat a woman much the same. The satisfaction on his face, as he stroked his Lady affectionately, melted me inside.

He put his head down as he strummed a few notes, his face hidden from my view. I wanted to tilt his head up so I could watch his face. The Lady was magic. Her music weaved a spell over me as I moved closer. The melody captured me, my hips swaying gently. My eyes closed as I felt the song wash over me. Was it the guitar working the spell or was he the magician?

I danced to the music, right in front of him. He couldn't help but see me dance. I stood with a long white dress on. My body moved to the sweet song coming from the Lady in his hands. I wanted to be that Lady. My hands roamed over my dancing body as the song continued. Eyes closed, I was one with the music.

Arms embraced me and spun me to the tune that now played on its own. Magic, pure magic and he was the magician controlling the spell. My hands slid across his cheeks, fingers buried into his hair. I pulled him toward me, kissing him full on his lips. They made my body sing with delight. His fingers rested on my hips, tapping gently, keeping in time with the music. The thought of him playing me turned me inside out.

As we danced cheek-to-cheek clouds filled the room. The enchantment sent us waltzing among the mists with the full moon streaking through, lighting our dance floor. He dipped me, kissing me just below my ears as his lips moved to capture mine.

His hands were splayed across my back, as they guided me close to him once more. He dipped me again, arching my body away from him, as only my hips touched his. I felt his arousal. He brought me back up again, pressing me full against him. He kept his arm resting on the small of my back, while his hand cupped my chin and he nipped my lower lip. I moaned softly and he smiled at me.

I wondered, could we make music together? My fingers wanted to stroke him, make sounds come from within while I touched his heartstrings. I caressed his chest, and started to remove his shirt. The dress I wore mysteriously disappeared.

He dipped me yet again, flicking his tongue over my breasts, first one then the other biting them playfully. His teeth bit into my erect nipple eliciting a cry of pleasure from my lips.

He pulled me against him hard, teasing my sensitive breasts with the soft hair on his chest.

He spun me away from him and for a moment I felt lost in the nothingness. Quickly he brought me back tight to his body. My hands wrapped around him as we moved together among the stars. His lips brushed my ear, his tongue flicked out for a taste sending a tingle through me, eliciting a shudder from my body. With a brush of his arm a cloud parts to reveal a platform of fluffy white. Together we fell on the cloud bed.

His hands roamed leisurely from my neck to my belly, memorizing every inch until he stopped on my hips. I moved closer to him. Raising his arm again, we were both naked. His hand came to rest on my right hip, fingers traced along my curves. His touches caused a momentary shiver. His hand came to rest over my right breast, his fingertips circling the areola and the pert nipple.

"Tonight we share the secrets, together we'll experience pleasure as our love, trust, and will become intertwined. Our flesh and soul will merge, unified in body, mind, intellect, intuition, and spirit. Are you willing, my Daria? Will you join me?"

I tremble at his voice. The sound was as sensual as his music and his words. How greatly I've longed for him. To find a man who will worship me as I worship him. I feared I'd always be alone.

His lips caressed mine as he pleaded with me, "Believe. I am here with you, let me show you the magic of my touch."

"Yes, please." I knew this was my choice. At first it was only a room with a guitar. The magic of dreams was like that. I had to decide. I leaned forward, my lips grazing him as my tongue flicked out tasting him. I deepened the kiss. He moved over me, taking my silent kiss as consent. No more words are needed.

Placing a leg between my knees to spread them apart, his hips came to rest against mine. I breathed deeply as his weight covered my body. I was ready for him. I needed him. "Fill me," I pleaded with my eyes and mouth.

Lips on mine, his tongue slid into my mouth as with a swift thrust he also slid deep into my core. Sensations overwhelmed me. He moved in and out, the both of us riding a wave of ecstasy. I cried out only to have my sound captured in his mouth. My hips moved in time with the rhythm he created. A symphony of movements reached to a crescendo, each thrust striking a new chord of pleasure.

He gripped my nipple between his fingers and tugged on it as he twisted it as his thrust increased. Klaas gripped my hands and started to move even harder and faster. My mind was overwhelmed by the immense pleasure as I moaned his name over and over again.

I could hear exactly how wet I was, but there was no time to be embarrassed about it. A powerful orgasm was slowly starting to rise. Leaning over me, he closed his eyes and lowered his head. I raised my head and met him halfway. His lips instantly met mine again. He sucked my lip into his mouth.

Hooking a leg over his hip, I rolled my hips. His fingers flexed against my skin. Breaking the kiss, Klaas stared down at me as he raised his hips a few inches. I pressed my palm to his cheek first and his eyes fluttered as he entered me again. His fingers slipped into my hair as he lowered his head. Klaas' lips brushed my chin, my cheek, and my ear. Warm breath fanned my skin as a drop of sweat dripped from his skin onto mine.

The pleasure was rising again. I could feel it building higher and higher. I clung to him as I crashed over the edge. Barely floating down from the high, I opened my eyes and held on as I was rocked by wave after wave of pleasure. Our bodies continued to move together, our eyes locked. Slowly we relaxed, his weight rested on my body, comforting me.

Chapter 4

Daria

The sunlight streaming in through the curtains woke me. Emptiness filled me as I felt the bed beside me. A sound startled me. I looked around to see where it came from. My eyes came to rest on my stereo. It was on.

The music reminded me of something so very powerful. It hit me then. This was the same music that played in my dream. I laid awake confused whether to believe it was real or all a dream.

It was at that moment that Klaas entered my room, wearing only a towel. "Sweet Daria, did you enjoy last night?"

"It…it was real?" I stuttered in response. It was too fantastical, too wonderful to be real. As I looked at him I realized he looked different in the morning light. "You look… human."

Klaas tilted his head at me before giving me a beautiful soft smile. "This is how I appeared in our dreams, is it not?"

"Yes, but yesterday you looked so different. Which is real?"

"Which do you prefer?"

I stood up, not caring that I was naked before this beautiful man. His eyes held a vulnerability, an openness that I knew he kept hidden. I reached up and cupped his face in my hands. "The one that is how you look when you're alone, with no one to like or dislike your appearance. I want to see you for you, my Sandman."

"You believe," he whispered as his eyes slipped closed. As I watched, sand seemed to pull away from his skin and retreat into his hands. Before me stood the man, the being that I met last night. His skin was so beautiful. It reminded me of liquid gold as I watched the sands flow.

He truly was the Sandman and I stood on my tiptoes as I captured his lips with mine. "I believe. You're the one I've always wanted. I wanted you to be real with every fiber of my being."

Klaas smiled against my lips. Pushing me up against a wall in my bedroom, he nipped at my lips playfully, "The fates gifted you to me and I will never give you up, my beautiful queen." Claiming my lips in a bruising kiss, he used his thumb to massage my bud, causing me to gasp in pleasure.

My fingertips traced his collarbone as I returned his passion filled kiss. His arm slipped around my waist to tug me closer to him. Breaking the kiss, I started pressing kisses along his jaw. My tongue flicked out to taste his skin, causing me to moan in pleasure.

My hands found the towel that kept him from me. I freed him and tossed the towel aside. I smirked when he lifted me up, his hands kneading my bottom. Wrapping my legs around his waist, I took him in my hands and guided him to my warmth as I moaned, "Yes."

Klaas

I groaned, a deep sense of possessiveness filling me as I drove my cock home and filled her completely. This was my female, my partner and soon, my Queen. Now would not be slow and sensual, now was all about claiming her as mine. Slow and sensual would be for later. Now was all primal need for she was my destined mate.

"You like that," she whispered.

I slammed a hand onto the to keep myself up. Goosebumps broke out over my skin. Pleasurable shivers raced down my spine as she continued to place kisses on my neck. I jerked when she bit down again a little harder than the first time. Her tongue flicked out to soothe the pain.

Her lips tilted up against my skin. And then she did something I never expected. The hand on my hip slipped around to my ass. She squeezed. A strangled gasp fell from my lips.

Her smile widened. "You have a very sexy ass," she whispered in my ear. Daria's hand slipped up my back a few inches. Leaning forward, I buried my face against the crook of her neck and breathed her in. Her hands slipped into my hair.

I pulled back to look at her. Before I could utter a word, she cupped my cheeks and pulled my lips to hers.

Her hands slipped to my shoulders again. She used her thighs as leverage to roll her hips. I gripped her ass and gave in to her body's request. My movements increased until we were both panting. Low moans fell from her lips. Her pussy started clenching around my cock.

Reaching between us, I found her clit and pinched it. Her body tensed and a second later she cried out as she came. I kept moving, drawing out her orgasm until she exploded again. In and out I moved, banging the wall, her nails digging into my back as she clung to me, her orgasm rising higher with each movement.

Crying out my name, she threw her head back against the wall as one last powerful thrust threw her over the edge into ultimate bliss, the tightening of her muscles pulling me with her into oblivion. After several moments, Daria kissed me deeply and said, "Good thing no one is on the other side of that wall."

"My love, soon enough I will make sure all the realms hear you scream my name in pleasure. I look forward to showing you all the pleasures to be held in the Dream Realm and in our home.."

Daria laughed as she nipped at my collarbone. "If your realm is so wonderful why do you visit this one so much?"

My mate was so perceptive. She would forever keep me on my toes. "I was lonely and looking for you."

"Oooo… good answer."

I chuckled as I slipped out of her, the smile she wore turning into a pout. Kissing that pout, I laid her on the bed before taking hold of one of her beautiful breasts and tasting the taunt nipple before me.

"Oh Klaas!" she moaned as she thrusted her nipple further into my mouth.

As I loved one breast, I teased and pinched the nipple of the other, quickly bringing her closer to another orgasm. Reaching down, I dipped my thumb into her slit before using it to tease her bud, while shoving several fingers into her moist warmth. The sound of her pleasure was one of the most beautiful sounds he'd heard in his long life. Before long her body started to vibrate in my hands as bliss claimed her once again.

When she opened her eyes and looked at me, I said heatedly, "I'm claiming and marking every bit of you as mine." As she laid on the bed before me, I looked deeply into her purple eyes and rasped, "The most beautiful sight in the world lies before me."

"An offering to do with as you please," she said suggestively as her legs wrapped around my waist and pulled me closer to her.

Parting her legs, I leaned down and licked up her juices before using my teeth to nip at her teasingly. I suckled her bud until once again she was on the edge, stopping just short of that passion consuming her, I moved up and kissed her deeply as once again I filled her tight pussy with my thick cock. The wondrous feel of her brought forth a moan from my lips. "My favorite spot in the world."

"My Klass," she sighed happily, holding me close. "My Sandman. My Dream King."

Moving slowly, I made sure to hit every one of her pleasure spots until she was begging me for more. Only then did I truly pound and thrust into her, giving her everything she begged for. Before long, orgasm after orgasm claimed her and still I held out. It was only until her vibrating walls clamped so very tightly onto my cock almost continually that I allowed myself to follow her into ultimate bliss. Moment after moment, her walls massaged and squeezed me dry.

Breathing hard we clung to each other as our bodies continued to hum with aftershocks. After many long minutes, Daria finally murmured to me as she started to drift off to sleep in my arms, "Yours, always and forever."

Kissing her softly, I closed my eyes as I held her close and whispered, "My everything!" before I joined her in slumber.

Chapter 5

Klaas

Several hours later after waking and showering together, we dressed. "I wish to show you more of my realm. It's filled with many wonders. I also wish to show you my nightmares. You have nothing to fear from them. You are their Queen."

"But Klaas, I'm a human. How can I be your Queen?"

My fingers gently moved her silken hair behind her ear as I answered, "You have always been destined to be Queen. You aren't just a human. When I found you and our bodies were joined as one, your destiny was tied to mine. My immortality became yours. Look at your wrists, my Queen."

I watched as she saw the rune for 'Dream' along with a crown adorning her wrists. I watched as she rubbed at them and realizing they were permanent, she smiled at me. I loved to see her smile, her eyes twinkling with joy. I vowed to see her smile everyday for eternity.

The thought that I would never again be alone filled me with such joy, I couldn't help but pull her close as I kissed her soft lips. "You'll never be alone, I'll forever be by your side as you're by mine. I love you, my sweet Daria, forevermore."

"You own my heart, my Sandman. You always have. I love you, too. Forevermore."

Taking her hand in mine, I asked, "Ready to go home?" I smiled as Daria nodded, briefly closing her eyes, only to open them with a slight gasp.

We found ourselves walking on clouds that were soft and beautiful. Slowly they began to part to reveal the most beautiful of park-like scenes. As we stepped into that scene, the grass beneath our bare feet was lush and soft. There were flowers and cherry blossom trees everywhere, filling the air with a wonderful aroma.

Pointing to a castle on the horizon, I told her, "That is our home, the center of all dreams." The softest of breezes caressed our skin and caused the cherry blossoms to float down like snow. The sounds of a babbling brook somewhere in the distance could be heard.

I found myself smiling as I watched Daria smile as she took in the beauty of dreams. It didn't surprise me that she hadn't resisted the truth of who I was. Our dreams had prepared her. These were the gardens I had built when I first dreamed of her. It was as beautiful as she was.

As we continued to walk down the path we heard the sounds of a flute. Turning down a gentle bend in the path, we came upon a man leaning on a nearby rock. We approached him as Daria whispered to me, "This man resembles some of the warriors I've seen in Asian movies."

I smirked, knowing she enjoyed watching those kinds of films. "Good day, Guardian."

The guardian stopped playing his flute and looked at me before quickly bowing to me. "My lord, I was not aware that you'd returned."

"This is your new Queen, my fated one."

The guardian showed a bright smile before he could quickly hide it. He closed his eyes momentarily and as he opened them he replied, "Welcome, my queen. I apologize for my brief disrespect. Welcome to our land. I'm known as Kio."

"It's wonderful to meet you, Kio. I look forward to getting to know you and all of the dreams that reside in these lands."

I watched as Kio stiffened before looking at me nervously. "What is it, Kio?"

"Nothing, my lord. I will leave you alone now." I watched with a narrowing of my eyes as he simply smiled and went back to playing his flute. Dismissing his slightly odd behavior, making note to have my Dream Magistrate look into it. Deciding to continue on the path, I guided Daria to continue on the path before us.

After a little bit we once again came upon a slightly varied guardian and this time he wasn't alone. With him stood a young girl. As we approached them, she said to me brusquely, "My lord, you were not expected today. What do you want?"

My eyebrow raised at her disrespectful tone. Taking hold of her neck, I showed her for the nightmare that she was as her appearance changed from that of a little girl to that of a dark demonesque creature. "Remember who your master is, Sharin.

You will not address me or my Queen in such a manner. It would be easy to return you to the land of nightmares."

"My lord, she means no harm." I looked at Lio as he bowed before me, his eyes never leaving Sharin.

"It would be wise if you spent more time with your brother and less time under Sharin's control, Lio."

"Of course, my lord," he said as he quickly vanished from before us.

With that I tossed Sharin flying into the clouds. Dusting my hands off, Daria's voice eased the tension within me. "Are you ok?"

"Of course. Sharin can be… difficult. We are attempting to turn old nightmares into dreams. The results have been mixed." Taking a deep breath I turned and looked at her, a small smile on my face. "I hope I've not frightened you."

Daria wrapped her arms around my waist as she tucked herself against me, my arms immediately going around her and holding her close. "It sounds to me as if you are trying to help them but like unruly children, they must be dealt with a firm hand."

I felt a smile grow on my face. She understood me as no other ever had. I was truly blessed. I placed a tender kiss on her forehead but before I could respond the air turned more ominous.

Lio and Sharin appeared before me. Despite refusing to look me in the eye, Lio carried a sword and moved oddly, almost as if he were a snake-like creature. Sharin looked a great deal less sweet. She was losing control of her nightmare visage. "Humans are not welcome." In response to her words, Lio turned into a dragon-like creature that growled and hissed at us.

Daria released a scream as vines had grown out of the ground and were wrapping themselves around her legs and body. With a snap of my fingers, the vines vanished and Daria moved behind me holding on to my clothing.

"That was foolish, Sharin. You attack your Queen and think I will just let that be. You forget your place."

"No, you forget. I'm a nightmare and shall always be a nightmare," she screamed at me.

I held my hand out and she flew towards me in a blur of movement. My hand wrapped around her neck as I looked into her hollow black eyes. "You dare to threaten your master? It's time for you to learn that even nightmares can fear for I am the master of nightmares and dreams. You exist because I allow it."

With a flick of my wrist I sent both of them straight to the dungeons of the Land of Nightmares. I knew I had changed as anger filled me and taking a deep breath I tried to calm myself down. I didn't want to scare my Daria. "She wanted to be a nightmare so badly, I sent her to the dungeons there. Lio stayed at her side so by her side he can remain," I explained with a sigh as I turned to look at Daria. "I'm sorry, my love. This was not what I wanted you to see."

"Hush. All I saw was you being the Master of Nightmares. It was actually quite sexy if you ask me."

"Was it?" I asked with a smirk as I leaned down to kiss her lips. She tasted delicious. "How about I show you the castle now, in particular, my chambers?"

"Yes, please."

Epilogue

Daria
Several Months Later

I could feel his presence. He was close, but I couldn't see him. I was in a large, open space. I wasn't sure exactly where. I was surrounded by thick, gray fog that threatened to choke me with each breath I took.

"Hello?" I yelled, but received no answer. I heard footsteps, but couldn't tell which way they were coming from. I could feel my heart start to pound. My body shivered from both fear and the sudden chill in the air.

The footsteps grew louder as they came closer and closer. "Who's there?" I yelled, but still no response. I then felt a hand slowly move up my arm and tightly grip my shoulder. My breathing became faster and heavier as I became completely consumed with fear. My heart was pounding so loud in my ears that I could barely hear the sobs and whimpers escaping my mouth.

Then, with a force that almost knocked me off my feet, the hand turned me around. First, only a tall, dark shadow stood before me. I slowly began to see what was in front of me as the fog cleared away from him. He was tall, over six feet and had short, black hair. His skin was slightly pale and his cheeks had a tinge of pinkish red in them. He had full, red lips, but what struck me most were his eyes. Dark red and seemed as though they pierced my very soul.

I was frozen as my mind raced, wondering what this man needed from me. Yes, I knew he needed me. Suddenly, I heard his voice within me, from my very soul. "Hush. No harm will come to you." A breathless whisper and all my fears instantly vanished. All I could do was gaze into those beautiful eyes. I suddenly felt the urge to go to him and let him take me.

As if my feet and legs had a will of their own, they slowly started taking me closer to him. The man leaned in to me and down to my neck. He inhaled deeply, taking in my scent. As he exhaled, he let out a soft moan as if he'd smelled the most wonderful scent in his life. His hands came up to my breasts, his thumbs rubbing against my nipples through the fabric of my tank top. I could feel them become hard as he took them between his thumb and finger and squeezed and pulled on them gently, making me gasp.

He lifted my shirt just above my breasts and seemed pleased that I wasn't wearing a bra. He bent down and took one mound into his mouth, teasing and flicking my nub with his tongue. My hands went to his head, pulling him to me. He slid his hand down my shorts, feeling the wetness through my panties. He took his mouth away from my chest and stared at me, enjoying the pleasure on my face.

He then pulled my panties aside with his fingers and started rubbing my clit. My gasps became moans, feeling the ecstasy welling up within my belly. I lifted my head so I was staring straight into his eyes. "I'm yours, my lord,"I whispered. My body ached to feel him inside me.

He continued rubbing my clit a few more moments before shoving his finger deep inside me. My legs became weak and I had to grab hold of his shoulders to keep from falling. He bent

33

down and once again took a nipple into his mouth, teasing it with his warm tongue, still shoving his finger inside me faster and harder. My moans became louder and my body stiffened just as I was about to explode my hot cum onto his hand. Before I could, he quickly pulled his hand out of my shorts sending waves of longing and disappointment flowing through me.

He brought his hand up to his nose, inhaling deeply then licking my juices off of it, smiling as he did so. I could see two pointed and very sharp looking incisors protruding from his gums. He then leaned down, kissed me softly, and said, "I will make love to you, my sweet angel. Soon." With that, he slowly started to fade away.

I was filled with disappointment and frustration. "NO!" I yelled. "Please, don't leave me!" but he was gone.

My eyes shot open and I was back in my bed. "Just a dream." I said as I rolled over to look at the clock. It was almost 6:30 am. I had to be up at seven to get ready for work so decided to just stay up. It wasn't the first time I had the dream.

As I stepped outside after getting dressed, I heard a voice behind me call my name but when I turned around there was no one. I huffed at my silliness. Without looking, I started to walk when I slammed into a hard wall of muscle. I froze and my heart started to pound. My eyes slowly looked up at the man in front me and my pulse began to slow as I became entranced by him. He pulled me close, his eyes never leaving mine. "Sleep, my love," he whispered in my ear as I was enveloped by darkness.

I sat up in bed and realized it had all been a dream. As I looked around at the unfamiliar room I was in, I found myself in a large bed with black, satin sheets. The room was small and there were very few items in it. As well as the bed, there was a large dresser and two bedside tables. The walls were painted a dark shade of purple and there were long black drapes covering two windows. The room was fairly dark except for two lit red pillar candles that were on the tables.

As my eyes adjusted to the darkness, I saw something out of the corner of my eye. I turned my head slightly and gasped as I realized the man from my dream was lying next to me. My Klaas and his games. I would never be bored with Lord of Dreams.

I smiled softly as the Master of Nightmares slept. There was something so beautifully mysterious about him. He looked so peaceful in his slumber. I didn't want to wake him but he fascinated me as no one else ever had.

He was on his back, head tilted slightly towards me. I watched his chest move up and down in a slow rhythm. He had on a tight red shirt that clung to his toned muscles, and black jeans. His lips looked so lush, I felt an urge to kiss them, to feel their softness on mine.

I reached over and swept a lock of his black hair from his brow. Then, slowly, I leaned over him, placing my lips on his for just a moment. Pulling away, a soft giggle escaped as I leaned in again and kissed him longer this time. My hand went to his cheek, caressing it as I continued to ply his lips with soft kisses. I wanted to stop but my longing for him wouldn't let me.

I felt him start to kiss me back. I was startled for a moment, but was quickly consumed with the pure passion emanating from him. His lips parted slightly and his tongue slipped out, lightly licking my lips. I gasped at the sensation and opened my mouth, wanting his tongue to invade it.

His hand slid up my leg to my waist, pulling me closer until I was almost on top of him. Our tongues danced together for what seemed like an eternity. My hand moved down his cheek and down his chest to his groin. I rubbed the growing bulge, feeling it stir beneath my hand. I could feel the wetness start so seep out from between my legs and my clit started to throb. My body ached for him. Wanting, needing to feel his manhood inside me.

As if understanding my desires, he pushed me onto my back. I loved how his body covered me so completely, always keeping me safe. We lay there for a long moment, embracing, kissing, our hands roaming. He sat up and started unbuttoning my shirt. He pulled me up so it was easier to slip off my shoulders and then he went to work on my bra. Unfastening it then pulling it free from my chest. My breasts fell slightly, my nipples stood erect as if happy to finally be free from their restraint.

He cupped them in his hands, caressing them, kneading them gently. Tweaking the nubs between his finger and thumb. He bent down and sucked one into his mouth, swirling his tongue around it then lightly grazing over it, alternating, one, then the other and back again. I felt like I was in heaven. The slightest touch of him made my skin tingle, my pulse race, and sent a fire coursing through me that only he could extinguish.

I felt like I was floating with all the different sensations that were flowing through me. I could feel the bulge in his pants pressing against me. Oh how I wished he would give it to me, but he continued his torture.

He slowly moved down my body, licking and nibbling, pausing to give my navel some attention. When he reached my pants, he undid them and I raised my hips so he could slide them and my thong off. Then he continued his journey down until he reached his prize. He stayed there, hovering inches away from my pussy. He just stared at it as if it were the most beautiful thing he'd ever seen. Each breath he exhaled made my clit throb. I wasn't sure how much more I could take. He then lifted my legs onto his shoulders and sucked my hard pebble into his mouth, licking it, teasing it with his tongue.

My moans and gasps filled the room as he slid a finger in my slit, then another. Sliding them in and out, coating his fingers with my juices. He flicked his tongue on my clit in rhythm with his fingers, moving faster and faster. I could feel the burning in my belly, my muscles tensed and I let out a long cry of great relief as my orgasm rocked my body from head to toe.

He crawled his way back up to my face, kissing me, letting me taste the sweetness of my juices on his lips and tongue. I needed him more than ever. I started working his shirt out of his pants. He sat up and took it the rest of the way off. He then got off the bed and took his pants off. I sat up and felt a tingle in my pussy seeing his beautiful cock pointing at me.

I couldn't take my eyes off of it. I reached out and wrapped my hand around it, slowly stroking, rubbing my thumb around the thick head. A drop of pre-cum oozed out of the tiny hole. My mouth began to water, wanting to taste it. Sticking my tongue out, I licked it off. He tasted so good and I wanted to taste more.

I continued pumping his shaft while I wrapped my lips around the head, sucking, swirling my tongue around it. Soft moans came from deep inside his throat. I slowly slid my mouth further down his cock, sucking a little harder, bobbing my head a little faster. I started massaging his balls, gently squeezing them, tickling them with my nails. His hand went to the back of my head and he started to fuck my mouth.

His moans became more urgent and he started bucking his hips wildly. He let out one loud moan and then I felt the warm stickiness of his cum shoot into my mouth. I continued sucking him, swallowing every bit. I didn't want to lose a single drop. When he was finished, he climbed back onto the bed and collapsed onto his back. I gave him a few minutes to rest before going back to work on him. I wasn't finished yet.

I leaned down and took him back in my mouth, my tongue swirling, my head moving up and down slowly. I could feel him stiffening. It gave me such a sense of control, knowing I did this to him. He only ever felt this way for me. When he was hard again, I got on top of him, straddled him and slowly lowered myself, feeling his massive member part my soaked lips and glide against my velvety walls.

I began rocking my hips, feeling him touch my most sensitive spot deep inside me and it drove me wild. I rode him faster and harder, reaching around to play with his balls, my tits bouncing around. He grabbed my hips and started thrusting into me with all his might.

He rolled us over so he was on top of me. He put his arms under my legs, lifting them more as he pounded into me with fierce passion. My screams and cries of pleasure echoed off the walls. He bent down and started kissing me hard, shoving his tongue in my mouth. All I wanted, all I needed was for this moment to last forever.

He fed my pussy his dick for what felt like forever and yet seemed all too short a time when we both exploded in ecstasy. My eyes closed, my head tilted back, it felt like the room was spinning, our bodies dripping with sweat, the only sound was that of our heavy breathing. My body felt like it was floating, it felt like I was in heaven.

Before too long, sleep found me. Dreams came and went in a senseless blur. The most vivid dream began with feeling as if someone had pressed their weight down on the bed beside me. The gentle feather soft graze of lips and eyelashes touched the side of my face and ear. A quick flicker of a tongue brushed against the subtle flesh of my neck. I felt myself stir lightly. The area between my thighs began to throb with a growing, heated intensity.

A soft whimper caught in my throat. Against the back of my thigh, I could almost swear I felt my seducer's erection. I decided I didn't want to wake up from this dream. His hand crept across my side until fingertips found my nipple. It became taunt and with his attention hardened to a small peak. The hard tip of his manhood teased the moist treasure that eagerly awaited him. With ease, he guided himself into me. I gasped aloud as every inch of him filled me. My eyes fluttered open as he began to move himself in and out, each thrust as hard and deep as the first. He seemed to be savoring every moment, as if he had looked forward to it.

"This isn't a dream..." he whispered in between deep breaths and quiet noises of his own. I felt his hot breath in my ear.

I felt my desire brimming, and it was damned near to boiling over. His hips moved in a slow, deliberate circle. A strong arm circled my waist as he then pulled me to him while his rhythm quickened. A hand, much larger than my own, grabbed a handful of my hair. I then craned my head back, looking up at his face. My entire body tightened as my orgasm washed over me. He pressed his face against my neck and cried out as he flooded me. I could feel him contracting inside of me with each stream while he grinded his hips as if to milk every last drop.

Covering the side of my face in kisses, we held each other. I didn't honestly know whether to tell him how much I loved him, or slap him senseless for waking me. In the end, of course, my love for him prevailed. Fate had spoken after all.

With a content sigh I turned in my lord's arms. Placing a soft kiss on his chin, I smiled as I told him, "I love our games, Klaas. They always end in the best ways. Did you have to wake me for another round, though? I was having the weirdest dream about Abraham Lincoln and zombies."

His laughter warmed my heart in the best of ways. "This is only the beginning, my Queen. I am your Sandman. We have eternity together. I will come to you every night in your dreams. I will take you places you've never been, show you things you've never seen." As he kissed me with an intensity that left me breathless yet aching for more, I knew that eternity with him wouldn't be enough. He was the other half of my soul and together we'd rule the Land of Dreams and Nightmares.

 **THE END**

40

About the Author

Euryia Larsen grew up thinking that what she was being told about the world was only part of the story. She loves myths both historical and modern and often sees the the possibility in 'what if'. A good romance with strong 'alpha' heroes and even stronger heroines that can be a partner for them are her favorite kinds of books. If the heroines are just a tad crazy, even better.

Euryia is a stay at home mom of two beautiful daughters, three crazy cats, three crazier dogs and a husband to round out the bunch. She deals with her fair share of issues while dealing with Fibromyalgia and other complications and as a result, she's finds an escape in books where there is always a happily ever after. She's always been creative and has written for herself as an audience for longer than she can remember.

I'd love to hear your thoughts on this or myths or books in general or even just a hello.

Check me out at
http://www.EuryiaLarsen.com
or feel free to email me at
EuryiaLarsenAuthor@gmail.com

Other Books by Euryia Larsen

Broken Butterfly Dreams

Standalone Novellas:

The Mobster's Violet

Clover's Luck

Touch of Gluttony

Halloween Darkness

Another Notch On Her Toolbelt

Sealed With A Kiss

Fate's Surprise

Midnight Rose

His Curvy Housemaid

Hello, Goodbye

The Dark Side (Dragon Skulls MC):

Saint

Beautiful Smile

Twisted Savior

Belladonna Club:

To Trap A Kiss

His Peridot

Zima Family:

Devil's Desire

Cursed Angel

Baranov Bratva:

Sinful Duty

Sweet Child of Mine

Menage Series:

Masked Surprise

Sweet Cherry Pie

Home on the Ranch

Perfect Storm

Curveball

Lonesome Shadows

Cursed Guardians

Love is Love Boxsets:

Menage A Trois

Affaire de Coeur

Not the Good Guy (Kazon Brothers)

with Kyra Nyx:

Kazon Brothers Box Set

The Dark

The Beast

The Villain

Saga of The Realms:

Power of Love – Prequel Novella (Paperback)

Power of Love – Prequel Novella (Free Ebook)

Bonded By Destiny

War of Giants

Printed in Great Britain
by Amazon